SIMON & SCHUSTER BOOKS FOR YOUNG READERS

An imprint of Simon & Schuster Children's Publishing Division

1230 Avenue of the Americas, New York, New York 10020

SIMON & SCHUSTER BOOKS FOR YOUNG READERS is a trademark of Simon & Schuster, Inc.

For information about special discounts for bulk purchases, please contact Simon & Schuster Special Sales
at 1-866-506-1949 or business@simonandschuster.com.

The Simon & Schuster Speakers Bureau can bring authors to your live event. For more information
or to book an event, contact the Simon & Schuster Speakers Bureau at 1-866-248-3049
or visit our website at www.simonspeakers.com.

Book design by Laurent Linn

The text for this book was set in Family Dog.

The illustrations for this book were rendered in watercolor and ink.

Manufactured in China

0519 SCP

First Edition

2 4 6 8 10 9 7 5 3 1

Library of Congress Cataloging-in-Publication Data

Names: Wells, Rosemary, author, illustrator.

Title: Max & Ruby and twin trouble / Rosemary Wells.

Description: First edition. | New York : Simon & Schuster Books for Young Readers, [2019] |
"A Paula Wiseman Book." | Summary: "Max and Ruby prepare for a new baby sibling—only to find out
they are getting two of them!"—Provided by publisher.

Identifiers: LCCN 2018040504 | ISBN 9781534443655 (hardcover) | ISBN 9781534443662 (eBook)

Subjects: | CYAC: Babies—Fiction. | Brothers and sisters—Fiction. | Rabbits—Fiction.

Classification: LCC PZ7.W46843 Tw 2019 | DDC [E]—dc23

LC record available https://lccn.loc.gov/2018040504

Max & Ruby

and

TWIN TROUBLE

ROSEMARY WELLS

A Paula Wiseman Book

SIMON & SCHUSTER BOOKS FOR YOUNG READERS

New York London Toronto Sydney New Delhi

Max's sister, Ruby, knew **all** about new babies.

Mama and Papa were going to have one.

"You can see for yourself, Max," said Ruby.

"There's a new baby in there!"

But Max knew Mama had eaten too many cookies.

He showed Ruby the cookie jar. It was empty.

"See!" Max said to Ruby.

Ruby explained to Max all about

where babies came from.

But Max didn't believe Ruby.

He knew where babies came from. Taxis!

Cousin Martha came home in a taxi.

So did Aunt Ida's baby.

Ruby brought out her Hannah the Howler doll.

"I helped Mama when you were a new baby!" said Ruby.

"So I know **everything** you have to do."

Max knew he was never, ever a new baby.

"Hannah's hungry," said Ruby.

She pushed Hannah's button. Hannah had a **big voice**.

Ruby filled Hannah's bottle with water.

"Watch, Max. This is how you feed a baby," said Ruby.

Hannah drank the whole bottle.

It went right through her.

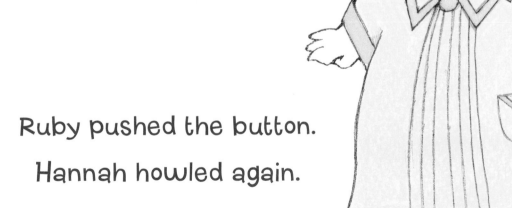

Ruby pushed the button.

Hannah howled again.

"Hannah needs a bath and a change, Max," said Ruby.

"Here's how you bathe a baby, Max. In she goes.

"Then you dry the baby off. On goes her nappy, then her nightie. Then you put her to bed. See?"

Hannah closed her eyes and went to sleep.

"Babies are **a lot** of work, Max."

Max could certainly see that.
He pushed Hannah's button.

"You woke her up, Max!" said Ruby.

"All done!" said Max.

Suddenly, it was time for the **real** new baby

to pop out into the world.

"It's going to be a girl. I just know it!" said Ruby.

Grandma came to babysit.

Grandma brought magic cards for Ruby.

She brought a space helmet for Max.

The next morning Max watched out the window.
"Taxi!" Max shouted. "Taxi!"

"**Oh my goodness!**" said Grandma.
"**Double wow!**" said Ruby.

There were **two**! Who knew?

Oliver was certainly not a girl.

"At least Grace is a girl," said Ruby.

Into the house the new family came.

Oliver ate and had his bath and got changed and went to sleep and woke up and ate again and had his bath again and went to sleep again.

Then Grace woke up and had her bath and her breakfast and her change and went to sleep, and then Oliver woke up.

Oliver had lunch. At naptime Grace woke up.

Day and night everyone worked.

Max wound up Oliver's and Grace's Vibra-Chairs.

Oliver grew bigger.   Grace began to sit up.

But one day Oliver and Grace both felt very peaky.
Nothing in the whole world made them happy.

Mama gave them gripe water.

Papa gave them a dab
of vanilla ice cream.

Grandma brought new toys.

Daddy changed Oliver.

Nothing worked!

Max wound up the Vibra-Chairs for them.

Everyone sang to them.

But no one could make Oliver happy.

Grace couldn't sleep.

No one could sleep.

Then Max had **an idea**.

He went into the toy box.

He pulled Hannah out from

under a pile of dolls.

He sat Hannah up in Oliver and

Grace's crib and pushed her button.

Hannah began to howl.

Oliver's little eyes lit up. Grace started laughing.

Soon, Oliver, Grace, and
Hannah fell asleep in a heap.
"All done!" said Max.